My Neighbour is a Werewolf

A Seriously Sam Story

Gloria Bompadre

Elena Porfiri   Glen Holman

My Neighbour Is A Werewolf

Written by Gloria Bompadre

Illustrations by Elena Porfiri & Glen Holman
Book design by Glen Holman
www.glenholman.com

My Neighbour

is a Werewolf

Next door, something
wasn't quite right…

strange noises came from
Mr Albert's house next door…

It was just past 9pm and a
full moon was shining. Sam was reading
scary stories in bed when he heard it…

Howling came from the neighbour's house.

Sam went to look out the window,
but he couldn't see anything...

He thought it was better go to sleep before his mum
realised he was still awake. He was still going to keep an
eye on the neighbour...

Mr Albert had moved next door a month ago, ALONE.
Sam had never spoken to Mr Albert
because he was NEVER around during the day.

The following morning, Sam tried to talk to Mum about the howling.

"Did you hear anything last night?" he asked.

"Like what?" replied Mum suspiciously.

"Like...*howling*?"

"I didn't hear any howling, don't be silly!"
cried Mum.

"Why does he live alone? He is strange."

"He is not strange because he lives alone! Get ready for
school."

Never mind, Sam was going to spy on Mr Albert. He
wanted to find out who his neighbour really was and
what the noise was all about.

There was a full moon shining again the next night. Sam waited for his mum to leave after reading his bedtime story. Then he put on:

Mask

Tights

Spy Belt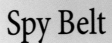

A Superhero / Spy / Detective costume — perfect for his mission.

Sam got to the window
and waited,

and waited,

and he fell asleep.

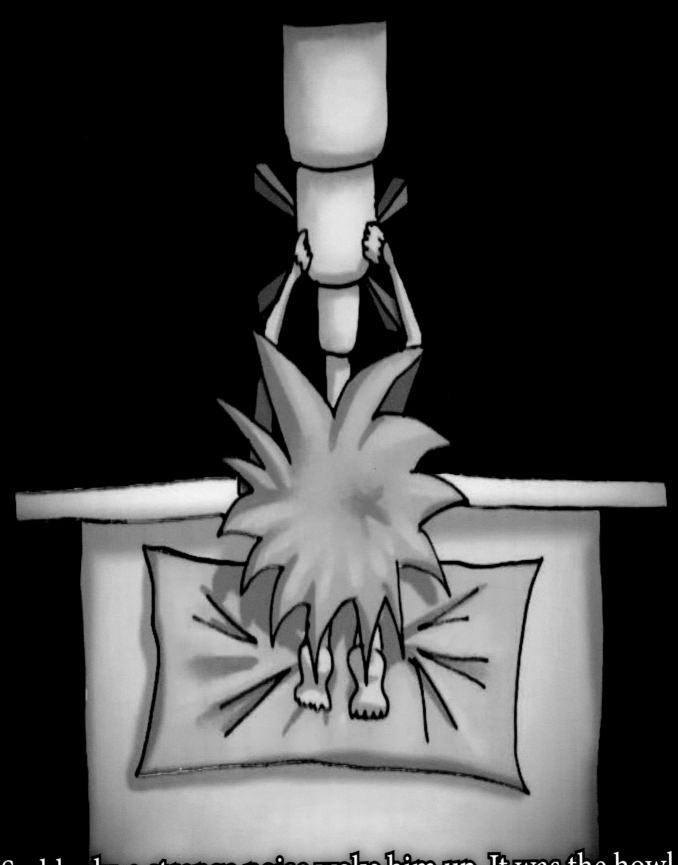

Suddenly, a strange noise woke him up. It was the howl again. Sam pointed the telescope to the neighbour's house and he SAW IT!

"What's going on?!"
asked Mum, running into the room.
"The neighbour is a werewolf!" yelled Sam.
"Look into the telescope!"

"What? NO! You mustn't spy on people,"
cried mum. "Are these my tights?"

Mum stayed with Sam until he fell asleep again.

Sam felt something sniffing and licking him.

It was IT! Mr Albert the werewolf!

Sam leaped over the fence
and sprinted straight to his mum.
"Hey! What's going on?" Mum yelled.

Mr Albert appeared over the fence
with the 'werewolf'.

"He fell in my garden," said Mr Albert.
"Fred must have scared him. He just wanted to
say hello, he's a friendly dog."

"But..." mumbled Sam, "you don't have a dog! We've never
seen a dog in your garden before!"

"Well, this is my girlfriend's dog," replied Mr
Albert. "She is a nurse and works most nights, so I dog sit.
I take him back to her in the morning,
so Fred isn't around much."

Sam was really embarrassed.
Mum was really angry.
"SERIOUSLY, SAM??!" yelled mum.
"Hey," said Mr Albert, "today is my day off and my girl-friend, Lucy, is coming here. Why don't you join us in the garden? And you can get in from the front gate..!"
"Thank you. We would love to," said Mum. "We just need to think about Sam's punishment before we come over."

"PUNISHMENT, WHY???"
"Well, let's see," said Mum.
"Late bedtime,
spying,

BREAKING INTO THE
NEIGHBOUR'S GARDEN!"

Sam had a BIG punishment…